John Swett, Charles Herman Allen, Josiah Royce

Bancroft's First Reader

John Swett, Charles Herman Allen, Josiah Royce

Bancroft's First Reader

Reprint of the original, first published in 1883.

1st Edition 2024 | ISBN: 978-3-38532-994-2

Verlag (Publisher): Outlook Verlag GmbH, Zeilweg 44, 60439 Frankfurt, Deutschland
Vertretungsberechtigt (Authorized to represent): E. Roepke, Zeilweg 44, 60439 Frankfurt, Deutschland
Druck (Print): Books on Demand GmbH, In de Tarpen 42, 22848 Norderstedt, Deutschland

BANCROFT'S

FIRST READER.

BY

CHAS. H. ALLEN,
Principal California State Normal School.

JOHN SWETT,
Principal Girls' High and Normal School, San Francisco;
Ex-State Sup't of Public Instruction, California.

JOSIAH ROYCE, PH. D.
Instructor in Philosophy in Harvard College.

SAN FRANCISCO:
A. L. BANCROFT & COMPANY.

A FEW WORDS TO THE TEACHER.

In General. There is no royal high-way to learning to read. No method, no device, no ingenuity on the part of the teacher can take the place of constant and prolonged drill upon the first few lessons, nor of the continued and attentive study of each succeeding lesson.

Intelligent teachers know that learning to read is, at first, but learning to recognize through the eye, what is already recognized through the ear. This book has been prepared with this thought constantly in mind. It does not, therefore, begin with words of two letters, nor with words having the same vocal elements in them. Children neither think nor talk in these words. On the contrary, words have been used, such as the child constantly uses. He is made familiar with these. With the phonic exercises, and the preparatory eye training, he will rapidly acquire the power to master other words.

Preparatory Drill.—Objects Before Words. It is not in the province of this book to prescribe, in detail, the preparatory drill which should be given before attempting to teach words.

The author earnestly recommends, however, that the first two weeks, at least, be entirely devoted to eye, ear, and voice training. The rapid recognition of objects held in the hand, of pictures, both on the blackboard and cut from books, will train the eye to see quickly and accurately; while questions about what is seen, descriptions of the things seen, and conversations about them, will give the pupil confidence in talking, and constitute valuable language lessons.

Pronouncing Lesson. All the new words occurring in a lesson are placed at the beginning, and should be carefully and thoroughly taught, before the child is required to *study* the reading lesson. This may be conveniently done in the following manner: At the close of each lesson, the pupil should be required to pronounce the words in the next succeeding lesson, receiving such aid as may be found necessary to secure the correct pronunciation of each word. The constant use of the blackboard is indispensable in teaching words.

Phonic Spelling. No apology is made for the prominence given to drill in elementary sounds in this and the other books of the series. The indistinct ·tones which render the exẽrcises in so many school rooms ·painful to the listener, still make one thing distinctly known—the need for regular and daily drills in elementary sounds. This work, therefore, is presented at frequently recurring intervals throughout the series, and in as great a variety of forms as possible. The teacher who, for a single term, faithfully takes up these exercises, will never again consent to forego them.

In the First Reader, the diacritical marks are introduced, primarily, as indications to the teacher of the sounds to be taught, and should be called to the notice of the pupil only when his observation has become quick enough to enable him to interpret readily their force; but the sound-training should begin at once, and should on no account be omitted or slighted.

Letters and Spelling. As soon as a few words have been learned by sight, it is well to teach a few letters each day as they occur in the new words, until all have been learned. To aid in this, the new letter forms of each lesson are introduced in this book separately, side by side with the phonic work. The alphabet will thus be almost imperceptibly taught, and can easily be reduced to order.

Great care has been taken to arrange conveniently for spelling, all the words used in the book. Let the child spell all the words of the lesson, at first with the book before him; but be sure he does it attentively.

Script Lessons. The script letters used should be taught by comparison with the Roman, and then copied on slate, paper, or blackboard. The script lessons, as well as the blackboard and slate exercises, are intended as suggestions for additional work to be given by the teacher, and are not designed to be exhaustive of the work which should be done.

Voice Training. Concert drill upon short poems and stories, and on colloquial phrases and sentences, is most excellent for teaching correct inflections, developing pure tones, and correcting errors in articulation; while at the same time it is a source of keen enjoyment to the child, rendering attractive his first days at school.

In this Reader the new sounds to be taught with each lesson, are indicated by letters printed in heavy type, with the diacritical marking. They are gradually introduced, and are taken from the words of the lesson. Words of the lesson composed of sounds previously learned are also introduced, to be spelled by sound; and if these exercises are properly taught, the ability of the child to pronounce new words, when he has finished the book, will be found surprising.

In Part I. of this Reader, diacritical markings of the new words at the head of each lesson, are placed on the long and short vowels only, and not on those until the sound marked has been specifically taught in the preceding lessons. Of the new words in Part II., all vowels are marked whose sounds have been previously taught.

The Script Lessons are designed to suggest the method of teaching, *not the* quantity to be taught. *A much greater number of lessons should be given than can properly find space in the Reader*

PART I.

1.

girl   hăt   dŏll

g

i

r

l

ă ŏ

LESSON 2.

a doll		a hat
the girl	and	the doll
the hat		a girl

h t

A T t	h-ă-t hat	n e h

A doll and a hat.

The girl and the doll.

The hat and the girl.

LESSON 3.

Năt   hăs   hĕn

n ĕ				
N	h-ĕ-n hen	N-ă-t Nat	s a

Nat has a hen.

The girl has a doll.

LETTERS AND SOUNDS ALREADY TAUGHT.

n   t   h   ă   ŏ   ĕ

ORAL BLACKBOARD WORK.

Show pupils how NEW *words may be formed, as follows:*

1. *By prefixing one sound to a combination of known sounds.*

t-ăn   n-ĕt   h-ŏt

2. *By annexing a sound.*

tĕ-n   tŏ-t   ŏ-n

3. *By combining single sounds.*

n-ŏ-t

Similar exercises throughout the book will assist the pupil to pronounce new words readily at sight.

LESSON 4.

căn

is

boy

nŏt

ball   See

| S b.d | e-ă-n   can   ă-n-d   and | C c o |

e   **d**

See the boy and the ball!

The boy is not Nat.

The boy can see the ball.

Can the girl see?

Can a doll see a ball?

LESSON 5.

dŏgs	boys	my	girls
Tăn	dŏg	good	I

My good dog.   The good boys.

ḡ   ĭ   ş̣

|M I| d-ŏ-ḡ dog ĭş is h-ă-ş has |m y|

The good boy has a dog.

My boys can see the dogs.

I can see the girls and boys.

My dog is Tan.

LESSON 6.—REVIEW.

H	h-ĕ-n hen	h-ă-s has
c-ă-n can	d-ŏ-ḡ dog	h-ă-t hat

Can I see the doll?

I can see the ball.

My good girl has a doll.

My good girl has a· ball.

See my dog and the hat!

Has the boy a hat?

The boy has a hat and a ball.

Can the boys see the ball?

Compare the script forms with the printed forms.

b *b*   l *l*   ġ *g*

boy   doll   girl

boy   *doll*   *girl*

LESSON 7.

căt
thĭs
răt
plāy
ĭn
bŏx
rŭn

r	ŭ			
x p u	r-ă-t	rat	r-ŭ-n	run

The cat can run.

This cat can play.

My cat can run and play.

Is the rat in the box?

Can the cat see a rat in the box?

The boy and girl see the rat.

LESSON 8.

Teach the script words by comparing them with the printed words.

boy   see   can

boy_____see_____can

Can   the   doll   see?

Can the doll see?

See   this   boy.

See this boy.

This doll can see.

This boy can see.

See this doll.

LESSON 9.

two cats
a red hen
Little Dora
a little ball

Dora	nāme	rĕd	wĭth
wĭll	lĭttle	two	she

ā m

D L w | r-ĕ-d red n-ā-me name

The name of the girl is Dora.
Little Dora has a red hen.
Dora will play with the hen.
She has two cats and a dog.

LESSON 10.

FOR PRACTICE IN SENTENCE READING.

The teacher should give the pupil a moment to look through the sentence, and then require it to be read as a whole, promptly.

This is a cat. | Can I see this cat? | See the good cat.

Can the cat see the boy? | The cat can see the boy.

See my good cat. | The little boy can play.

The rat can run. | The rat can run and play. | The dog has a rat.

REVIEW OF CONSONANTS.—SEPARATING FIRST SOUNDS.

d	d-ŏḡ	d-ŏll	e	e-ăt	e-ăn
h	h-ĕn	h-ăt	t	t-ăn	t-ŏp
r	r-ăt	r-ŭn	n	n-ăt	n-ŏt

LESSON 11.

rŭns   fĕnce
you   what
now   gō
ŏn   t●

ō l
ō-l-d old

p
p-ĭ-ḡ pig

See the pig run!
The pig runs to the old fence.
The dog plays with the pig.
Now the dog has the pig.
The pig will go to you.
What is on the fence?

LESSON 12.

	ŏŏ	
ĭ-n in	g-ŏŏ-d good	ĭ-ş is

*This lesson is to be read by filling each blank
with the name of some object above.*

Dora is in this —.

The girl has a —.

The boy has a — and a —.

This is a good____.

Is the cat in the____?

Can the hen see the____?

LESSON 13.

Kĭtty · looks

her　　　　　　　　　　Māy

fly　　　　　　　　　　ăt

for　　　　　　　　　　ĭt

---

k

| K   k | k-ĭ-t   kit | ă-t   at |

Do you see this cup?

It is for little May.

What is on the cup?

A fly is on the cup.

Kitty looks at the fly.

EXERCISE IN SHORT VOWEL SOUNDS.

ă	e-ă-t	c-ă-n	ŏ	ŏ-n	n-ŏ-t
ĕ	r-ĕ-d	h-ĕ-n	o͝o	l-o͝o-ks	g-o͝o-d
ĭ	p-ĭ-ḡ	ĭ-n	ŭ	c-ŭ-p	r-ŭ-n

LESSON 14.—SLATE LESSON.

See the pig look!

He looks for May.

What has May for

the pig?

Now the boy runs.

Can I run to you?

See me run, May.

This is my box.

A fly is on the box.

Now see it fly.

LESSON 15.

do

we

băd

trăp

says

Dĭckie　　come　　nice　　mamma

b	ū
|RO| b-ă-d bad　t-r-ă-p trap　ū-se use	

"Come, mamma, do come!" says
Dickie Rat. "See this little box.

"May I go in it to play? It
is a nice box to play in."

"O no, Dickie! it is a trap.
We will not use it."

LESSON 16.

The girl has a

The girl has a

See this

See this

A good

A good

See my

See my

A —— and a boy.

A __ and a boy.

This good ——.

This good

LESSON 17.

ha !　　duck　　corn　　păn

hăve　　fast　　here

v	th	s
v	h-ă-ve have	th-ĭ-s this

Come here, come here, little duck!

See what I have in this pan.

Corn is good for little ducks.

Can you run, little duck?

O, see it run, ha! ha! ha!

The little duck can not run fast.

LESSON 18.

mē	gĕt	out	po͞or
ride	gĭves	Dăsh	wants

o͞o		ē	
P	p-o͞o-r poor	m-ē me	

Dora gives Kitty a ride.

Kitty will not ride fast.

Dash will not run with Kitty.

Kitty looks at me.

Poor Kitty wants to get out.

She wants to run and play.

LESSON 19.

ī

r-ī-de   ride   l-ī-ke   like

FOR PRACTICE IN SENTENCE READING.

The teacher should give the pupil a moment to look through the sentence, and then require it to be read as a whole, promptly.

Come here! | Look at me.

I ride fast.

I ride with mamma.

This is a bad rat. | Can the rat get out?

The cat wants the rat.

ORAL BLACKBOARD WORK.

EXERCISE COMBINING KNOWN SOUNDS IN NEW WORDS.

m	n	t	ā	ă	c	p	ī	ĭ	ŏ
		s	ĕ	b	ḡ	ŭ			

m-ă-n   m-ā-ne   t-ĭ-n   t-ī-ne
t-ă-p   t-ā-pe   s-ĕ-t   s-ĭ-t
m-ĕ-t   f-r-ĕ-t   m-ŏ-p   b-ŭ-ḡ

LESSON 20.

Oral lessons for sounds of

sh   ch   wh

sh - - shall

sh - - show

hu - - sh

ch - - chill

ch - - chin

wh - - why

wh - - what

wh - - white

LESSON 21.

ŭp   Tŏm   hĭs
ŏff   līke   Dăn
fŭn   see-saw

f

f-ŭ-n   fun

Tom and Dan can have a ride.

The boys like to see-saw.

Tom is up and his hat is off.

What fun the boys have!

I like to see Tom and Dan ride.

REVIEW EXERCISE IN CONSONANT SOUNDS.

b	b-ăd	b-ŏx	t	T-ŏm	t-răp
p	p-ăn	p-ĭg	f	f-ŭn	f-ast
d	D-ăn	d-ŏg	v	hă-ve	

LESSON 22.

Bŭttercŭp

Maud cow

hănd pĕt

nĕck bĕll

Nĕd

	ē̃		
B	h-ĕ̃-r her	h-ō-me home	

Buttercup comes home with Maud. She is a nice little cow.

Can you see the bell on her neck?

Maud has her hand on Buttercup.

Ned has a pet cow.

LESSON 23.

ŭnder

love

hĕld

put

said

tōō

yĕs

Y

"Do you love butter?" said mamma.

Dora put up her chin, and mamma held a buttercup under it.

"Yes, yes," said mamma, "my little girl loves butter."

"You love butter too, mamma," said Dora.

LESSON 24.

PRACTICE IN SENTÉNCE READING.

The teacher should give the pupil a moment to look through the sentence, and then require it to be read as a whole, promptly.

Can you see me? I can see you. Here is a buttercup for you.

Will you come in? Yes; I want to see you. Give me your hat.

See my pet dog. Do you like dogs? No, I like cats and hens.

ORAL BLACKBOARD WORK.

Show the pupil how NEW *words can be formed by combining the letters as given below, with the long vowel sounds,* ā, ē, ī, ō, ū, ōō.

ne   t   **me**   g   **ld**   m   **n**

d   s   p   **re**   **ak**

Examples.—t-ā-me   d-ī-ne   p-ŏ-s-t.

LESSON 25.

dĭshes·

small

tāble

·they

tĭn

Grāce   hăppy   sĕt

| G | th-ĕ-m them   s-ĕ-t set   ŏ-n on

Grace has come tᴏ see May.

May has a set of small dishes,
and a table to put them on.

Grace has little tin dishes. I
can see them in the box under
the table.

LESSON 26.

chĕrries săng there

rīpe
awāy
birds
keep

ä	**ạ**	
ä-re are	ạ-ll all	b-ạ-ll ball

"Cherries are ripe, cherries are ripe," sang the birds one day.

"Cherries are ripe," sang the boys and girls.

"Now for fun," said the birds.

"There are cherries for all," said mamma.

LESSON 27.

nŭts

ēat kīnd

one dēar

why your

afrāid Bŭnny squirrel

| q | h-ĭ-t hit k-ī-n-d kind n-ŭ-t-s nuts |

I see you little squirrel. Do not run; I will not hit you.

What is your name? Bunny?

Do you like nuts, Bunny?

Come here, I will give you one.

Dear little Bunny, why are you afraid? I am kind to all my pets.

LESSON 28.

FOR PRACTICE IN SENTENCE READING.

The Teacher should give the Pupil a moment to look through the sentence, and then require it to be read as a whole, promptly.

What is your name?

My name is Dora. What is your name?

My name is Maud. Do you play here?

Yes, I play here all day. I have a low table and some tin dishes.

I have a doll and a squirrel. He eats nuts, and we eat cherries.

REVIEW OF VOWEL SOUNDS.

ā	n-ā-me	ă	ă-nd	ī	r-ī-de	ŏ	ŏ-n
ä	ä-re	ē	sh-ē	ĭ	ĭ-t	û	û-se
a̤	a̤-ll	ĕ	p-ĕ-t	ō	n-ō	ŭ	ŭ-p

LESSON 29.

lose

săd

ĕgg

tree

hŭsh thēse their

rĕst tāke would

Hush! hush! Do you not see the birds? Their nest can not be very far off.

Oh, I see the nest. It has an egg in it.

I will not take the egg. The birds would be sad to lose it.

LESSON 30.

Clăra   fōur   sāme   class

bĭg   about   rēads   vĕry

Here are four little girls and two big ones.

They are all in the same class.

What are they reading? Is it about Maud?

Clara is reading now. She reads very well.

LESSON 31.

gōing ĭf
Jŏhn ăm

tīme

kīte

tāil

hĭll

J	ng
l-ŏ-ng long	s-ă-ng sang
h-ĕ-l-p help	ḡ-l-ă-d glad

O, John, what a nice kite!
What a long tail it has.

The tail may be too long. It
will not fly if it is.

Are you going to fly it?

Yes; I am going to the hill.

LESSON 32.—UP I GO.

Up I go, up I go,
See me, see me, ho, ho, ho!
If I see a fly go by,
I can hit him if I try.

I see a fly, I see a fly,
Up, up he goes into the sky,
I will not try to hit the fly,
No, little fly, by-by, by-by.

if   hit   try   goes
sky   by-by

LESSON 33.

sō   nēar   whĭch
ly   pu   never
stănd
taller
sīze
Jāne
tōes
Anna

| F z |

Which is the taller, Jane or Anna?

They are near the same size.

O Anna, you are standing on your toes.

What a sly puss you are! Jane would never do so.

LESSON 34.

bāby

bābies

crĭb

ŏdd

tĕll

bĕst

hŏŏd

| **z** | |
| s-ī-ze　size | wh-ĭ-ch　which |

Two babies in one crib! How odd to see them!

Which do you like best, the one with the hat, or the one with the hood?

I like the one with a hood.

LESSON 35.

Mĭss

sŭch

how

dŭll

Māry　tēacher　whĭps　many

s-ŭ-ch such   d-ŭ-ll dull   b-ĕ-s-t best

This is the teacher, Miss Mary.
She has four dolls in her class.
They must be bad dolls. See
how many whips she has.

I would not like to teach such
a dull class.

LESSON 36.

tēa

bĭts

thăt

pāys

buy

down

shawl

căndy   Sălly   fŭnny   some

s-t-ō-re store b-ĭ-t-s bits l-ī-ke like

May and Sally are playing at store.

May keeps the store. Sally has on her mamma's hat and shawl, and comes to buy of her.

Sally says she would like a very little good tea, an egg, and some candy.

Does not Sally look funny, with that shawl on?

LESSON 37.

mother
clēan
dirty
lŏoked
water
queen
drĕssed
sōld

washing   clōthes
sōak   whĕn

When May and Sally had sold out their store, May said, "O

mother, may we have a washing day?"

"A washing day! why do little girls want a washing day?"

"My doll's clothes are so dirty,
we want to wash them," said
Sally.

" O, then you may wash them,"
said mother.

When the doll was dressed in
her clean clothes, she looked like
a little queen.

WORD BUILDING.

*The teacher should give additional words containing
the following combinations of letters:*

th	sh	wh
th-e	sh-ow	wh-at
th-is	sh-all	wh-ich

LESSON 38.

pert	frŏg	dared	fēar
wŏn't	dōn't	stĭll	master
lĕft	fīnd	bow-wow	hĭm
now	row		lŏg

I.

A pert little frog
    Sat under a log,
And dared not come out,
    For fear of the dog.

II.

The dog said, "Bow-wow!
    O do come out now."
"I wŏn't," said the frog,
    "So don't make a row."

III.

Then off went the dog,
    And left master frog;
And there you may find him,
    Still under the log.

LESSON 39.—REVIEW.

May has a nice box for her doll and her doll's clothes.

The baby likes to play with May's box, but, to-day, May will not let him. She says baby is too little to play with dolls.

May is not a bad little girl. She loves baby, and when he is dressed clean and nice, she likes to take him to ride.

It is too bad she will not let him play with her now.

The teacher will find in the Second Part, the equivalent vowel sounds gradually introduced for practice as they occur in words of the reading lessons, upon the same plan of systematic phonic training, which has been employed in the preceding pages. These lessons are carefully arranged in easy grades, and should be thoroughly taught.

ROMAN ALPHABET.

A a	I i	Q q
B b	J j	R r
C c	K k	S s
D d	L l	T t
E e	M m	U u
F f	N n	V v
G g	O o	W w
H h	P p	X x
	Y y Z z	

FIGURES.

1 2 3 4 5 6 7 8 9 0

SCRIPT ALPHABET.

SCRIPT FIGURES.

PART II.

KATY ON HER WAY TO SCHOOL

1. JOHN AND PRINCE.

lēave	Prĭnce	cạlls	basket
nămed	horse	ăpples	sōōn

> **ea** = ē
> l-ea-ve   leave   n-ā-me-d   named

Prepare the pupil to recognize silent letters by frequently asking him to notice that a word has more letters than it has sounds.

1. John has a fine horse. His name is Prince.

2. Prince is very fond of apples.

3. John takes a basket of apples, goes down to the fence, and calls: "Prince! Prince!"

4. Then Prince runs up to the fence, and eats all the apples. He does not leave one.

5. John has a very wise dog named Don. Don is a good dog, and does what John tells him.

6. When Prince is far off, and can not hear John call, he says: "Go get him, Don."

7. Don runs away as fast as he can, and soon drives Prince to the fence.

8. John is always kind to Don and Prince.

2. JENNY DILL.

rĭll   dŏt   tŏt   cŏt

In a cot on the hill,
Lives little Jenny Dill:
She is but a tot,
As big as a dot,
And a shy little tot is she.

She sits by the rill,
She runs on the hill,
She is but a tot,
As big as a dot,
But the shy little tot loves me.

WORD BUILDING.

-ing

play-ing	**look**-ing
work-ing	**go**-ing
eat-ing	**rid** (e)-ing
tak (e)-ing	**hav** (e)-ing

3. THE RAIN.

thănk

warm

ōver

green

rāın	brīght	͵sĭng	flowers
wĕt	joy	māke	wāy
schōol	pŏnds	rōad	sīde

th n = ng

th-ă-n̲-k   thank   s-ĭ-ng   sıng

1. See the rain come down!
It will wash all the leaves, and
make them bright and green.

2. The little flowers will all look up glad and happy, as if they would say, "Thank you!"

3. These children, on their way to school, will be very wet by the time they get there.

4. When the rain is over, the sun will come out bright and warm, and the birds will sing for joy.

5. Boys and girls have good fun when it rains, playing in the little ponds by the road side.

6. When they get home, their mamma will say, "O children, you are so wet! I fear you will have a chill." The children will say, "O mamma, it is such fun; never fear for us."

4. GEORGE'S RIDE.

grass	hĕads	jŭst	lĕgs
papa	tŏok	thōse	tŏld
tīred	wīld	was	were
drēamed	first	fōod	. George

e-r-ĭ-b crib dr-ĕa-m-ed dreamed

1. George took a ride with his papa and mamma one day when he was four years old.

2. It made him wild with joy when he saw the trees and grass.

3. He saw, too, for the first time, some ducks on a pond.

4. Papa let him take a good long look at them.

5. Just as he was looking he saw two of the ducks put their heads under water.

6. "See, mamma!" said George, "the little ducks are eating their legs."

7. Mamma said, "No, they are not eating their legs, but looking for food."

8. On the way home the little boy was very still, for he was very tired.

9. As soon as he was nicely in his crib, he went to sleep and dreamed of little ducks.

5. THE KETTLE.

other	lärge	kĕttle	chĭckens
boil	hŏt	friĕnd	cŏffee-pŏt
		voıce	lärgest

1. I am a kettle. I boil water for your tea. When I get hot, I sing for joy.

2. This is my friend, the coffee-pot. He has no voice, and can not sing.

3. Here you see my other friends. They look like a hen and her little chickens. The largest one is the tea-pot. I love her best of all.

6. REVIEW.

ȯ = ŭ

ȯ-th-er other	l-ȯ-vc love

1. These children are riding in the rain. Are they on their way to school?

2. No, they are going to see their kind teacher, Miss Maud.

3. She likes to have John and Grace take tea with her.

4. When the kettle sings, John says it is like a fat little man.

5. Miss Maud sits down and lets Grace make the tea and set the table.

6. There is no fun for the children like taking tea with their teacher.

7. A BEAR IN SCHOOL.

ĕver	blăck	brĕad	dōor
bear	dĭnner	hŭ<u>n</u>gry	öpened
rōsy	āte	wạlked	wĕnt
	önly	wạnted	

---

ee = **ē**   **ch** = **k**

ch-ee-şe cheese   s-ch-ōō-l school

th-ĭ-<u>n</u>-k think

---

1. Did you ever see a big black bear? This one came to school one day.

2. He was hungry and wanted some dinner.

3. What do you think he ate? The boys and girls?

4. O no, he only went to their baskets, and ate their bread and butter, and rosy apples.

8. WHICH IS THE BEST?

crīed	mĭlk	ūse ful	cŏck	thĭngs
puss	bōne	bōast	frŏm	thăn
mew	ĕvery	mornıng	thiêves	wăken
mōre	lāy	should	house	clŭck
		watch	nīght	

1. "Cock-a-doodle-doo!" cried the cock; "How useful I am! I get up first in the morning, and waken all in the house."

2. "Cluck! cluck! cluck!" said the hen; "I am more useful than you. Every day I lay a nice egg for my master."

3. "Mew! mew! mew!" cried the cat; "I keep the rats and mice from the bread and cheese."

4. "Bow! wow! wow! wow!" said the dog; "I watch the house at night, and keep away the thieves. My master can not do without me."

5. Just then the master came out. He gave corn to the hen and cock, milk to puss, and a bone to the dog.

SCRIPT WORK.

Copy these sentences on your slates, to read in class.

1. The cat can catch rats and mice.

2. Hens lay eggs, and eggs are good to eat.

3. A good watch-dog is useful to his master.

4. The master fed all of them, for they were all his friends.

5. We should all try to be useful, and we should not boast.

9. THE OWL.

By Sound.
Word-building.

ăs

dăy

eyes ·

owl

dŏes

stăy

ow

h-ow

n-ow

c-ow

d-ow-n

b-r-ow-n

$$\bar{y} = \bar{i}$$

s-ĭ-t-s   sits   f-l-ȳ   fly   t-r-ee   tree

1. I see an old owl,
    As he sits in the tree;
I see his big eyes,
    But he does not see me.

2. Up there he will stay,
    In the tree, all day;
But when night comes,
    He will fly away.

10. JUMBO AND BABY.

băg	care	around	härm
trŭnk	răther	pēa-nŭts	Jŭmbō

ea – ĕ

d-ĕa-d dead p-ĕa-n-u-t-s pea-nuts

1. Here are Jumbo and Baby.
Is it not an odd baby? Its mother
is dead, and good old Jumbo takes
care of it.

2. How kind he is! See how he puts his trunk around it to keep it from harm.

.3. Good Jumbo! you and Baby shall have a bag of pea-nuts, or would you rather have candy?

11. LITTLE ROBIN.

twĭg

rŏbin

seem

hŏp

skȳ

O robin, little robin,
    You sit up on a twig;
You seem so very little,
    And I so very big.

But, robin, little robin,
  You can fly up in the sky;
I can not, little robin,
  I can not, if I try.

And robin, little robin,
  You can hop from twig to twig;
I can not, little robin,
  If I am so very big.

Well, robin, little robin,
  Hop and fly, hop and fly,
Be happy, little robin,
  Be happy, so will I.

12. REVIEW.

$ay = \bar{a}$

d-āy day   c-ā-k-es cakes

1. One day a man came by the school with two bears.

2. Miss Mary let the children go out to see them.

3. One bear was black, and one was brown. The man put his hat on the brown bear, and it walked on two legs.

4. The children all laughed to hear it try to sing.

5. They were afraid to go near the bears, but they gave the man apples and nuts for them.

Copy and fill the blanks.

One bear was ——— and one was

13. THE ORANGE GIRL.

fäther

ëach

shôrt

mŭch

yēar

hăd

lóved

ŏranges

brȯther

befōre

agō

sēa

mĕt

any

new

shĭp

răgged

ô = a̤

ô-r or	f-ô-r for	l-ȯ-vc-d loved
sh-ĭ-p ship	s-ēa sea	c-ȯ-me come

---

1. "Oranges! Oranges! Buy my oranges!" sang a ragged little girl.

2. A short time before, she had come in a large ship from over the sea.

3. Her father and mother are dead. She came here to find her brother, who left home many years ago.

4. One day her brother met her in the street, and took her to his new home.

5. Then she was never sad any more.

Jack Dora Grace Clara
Susie Maud Ned Tom
Willie Belle Anna Harry

Miss Grey Miss Maud
Miss Brown Miss Mary

14. DOT, THE MONKEY.

tríed

sŏrry

pulled

fĕllow

tōoth-āche

mónkey

trĭcks	fạll	last	săt	nēat
fȧce	pāin	strĭng	tīed	pạw

> ## ai = ā
> p-l-ȧy play   r-ȧi-n rain   t-ōō-th tooth

1. Dot is a monkey. He is a happy little fellow, full of play and tricks.

2. But last week, Dot was not happy. He had the tooth-ache.

3. He sat on the mat, put his paw up to his face, and cried. Did you ever see a monkey cry?

15. JOHN AND KATE.

shīne   wĭn   trīes   rŭnning
    sĭster   rāce   ạlwăys

$$\breve{y}=\breve{i}$$ $$\hat{a}$$
n-ẽa-r near   s-t-ō-r-y̆ story   c-a-re care

1. What fine fun John and Kate seem to have.

2. They are running a race to the fence.

3. See how Kate's eyes shine! I think she is going to win.

4. Look out, look out, John! or you will be left.

5. It may be that John is not running very fast, so that his little sister can be first.

16. KATE AND HER PET CAT.

Pĭnk
scrătch
fīre
drȳ
gone
blāze
hẽard

rōōm   hīde   frĭght   seek   greāt

1. Kate has a pet cat named Pink.

2. Pink is full of fun and can play hide-and-seek with the children.

3. But one day Pink was very useful, too. I will tell you how it was.

4. Kate's mamma had left some clothes by the fire to dry, and had gone out.

5. Before long, Kate heard Pink scratch the door, and mew, as if in great fright.

6. She ran into the room, and there were the clothes all in a blaze.

7. Now Pink is more of a pet than ever.

17. A PICTURE LESSON.

Question the children about this picture. Ask them to tell what the little boy is doing; what he has on his head; how it looks; what he meets in the road; what they think his name is, etc. Afterward, if they can do it, let them write out the story for themselves.

18. THE FROG AND THE MOUSE.

jŭmp   tīe   răn   untĭl

stŏp   mouse   rĕady

j

j   j-ŭ-m-p   jump

1. One day a little mouse ran away to play with a frog.

2. O, what fun they had! They played see-saw until they were tired out.

3. At last, the frog said: "Tie

your foot to mine, and I will teach you how to jump."

4. "That will be fine," said the mouse, and away they went, till they came to the pond.

5. "Now," said the frog, "make ready; one, two, three, and—"

6. "Stop!" cried the mouse.

7. But it was too late, and the frog laughed till he cried, as the little mouse went down, down, down, under the water.

Copy, and fill the blanks.

Poor little ____ mouse! Do you think it was ____ ? Was it not a bad ____ to laugh at ____ ?

19. TOMMY AND HIS SISTER.

cāne

tēase

sūre

rīght

plāything

häll-wây

Tŏmmy   Jŏnes   flōor   hănds

ou	a͟ = ŏ
f-ou-n-d found	wh-a͟-t what

1. Tommy Jones had a box of playthings, and was playing with his sister on the floor.

2. He soon got tired, and then what did he do?

3. He found his papa's hat and cane in the hall-way, and just see what he is doing.

4. He is trying to put the hat down over his little sister's head.

5. Do you think he is a kind brother to tease his sister in this way?

6. It may be fun for him, but I am sure she does not like it. She puts up her little hands to stop him.

7. Why do you not ride your cane, Tommy, and play horse? That would be all right.

8. Good boys do not tease their little sisters, but are always kind to them.

Copy, and fill the blanks.

Good —— do —— tease —— little sisters, but —— always —— to them.

20. WHAT I DO.

Mȯnday	Tūesday	fâir	Wĕdnesday
nȯthing	blōws	īron	Thursday
Frīday	sweep	sew	Sŭnday
sīght	chûrch	ĕlse	Săturday
work	cŏŏk	dŭst	ạlthōugh
	bāke	knĭt	

1. On Monday, when the day is fair, I always wash the clothes.

2. On Tuesday, I can iron them, although it rains and blows.

3. On Wednesday, I sew and knit and always like it, too.

4. On Thursday,

I can see my friends, I've nothing else to do.

5. Then Friday is the time to sweep; to dust and set things right.

6. On Saturday, I bake and cook, and then put all work from sight.

7. And Sunday, is a day of rest; I go to church dressed in my best.

û

w-a-sh   wash   .   ch-û-r-ch   church

Copy, and fill the blanks.

On Wednesday, I —— and ——.

On Saturday, I —— and ——.

21. LITTLE MABEL.

Măbĕl

äuntiĕ

bŏnnet

frĕsh

Hărry

brīght

sŭnny

yärd

nīcer   sĭck   mŭst   cŏat   to-dāy

fĭll   knōw   hōpe   grōwing

ĩ=ẽ

f-r-ĕ-sh fresh   g̃-ĩ-r-l girl   h-ẽ-r her

---

1. See this little girl. She has been sick for a long time.

2. This is a bright, sunny day, but she must have on her coat

and bonnet to go out in the yard.

3. How glad she seems to be out of doors to-day.

4. The grass is fresh and green, and she wants to fill her little hands with it.

5. Flowers, too, are growing in the grass. She will get some I am sure, to take to her mamma.

6. Do you want to know her name? It is Mabel, but her big brother Harry calls her Bell, which is a much nicer name for a little girl.

7. Her auntie lives near, and has sent for Mabel to come and take tea. I hope she can go, for she is a good girl.

22. SUSIE'S LETTER.

Sŭsĭe

côrner

where

lĕtter

wāit

rēach

wrīting

who

stĕps

been

---

u̧ = oŏ

p-u̧-t   put   s-e-r-ă-t-ch   scratch

---

1. Here is little Susie, who has been writing a letter to her papa.

2. She has run away from

home to put it in the letter-
box.

3. But now she is there, she
can not reach the box, and does
not know what to do.

4. She can run home and tell
mamma about it; her house is
just around the corner, where
you see the steps.

5. I think her papa will be
very glad to get the letter, even
if he can not read it.

6. This is about the way it
will look.

23. NANNY.

päth	pătter	pōrch	cạught
lămb	clătter	Nănny	acrŏss
feet	härd	Jōe	tēars
stŏŏd	agaın	wŏŏd	bụshes
	ōwn		

---

p-ä-th   path   h-ä-r-d   hard

1. "Patter! patter!" came four small feet up the hard path.

2. "Clatter! clatter!" came the feet across the porch.

3. "There's your sheep, Joe," said May.

4. "Why, Nanny," said Joe, "how did you come here?"

5. "Ba-a-a!" said Nanny, and the tears almost stood in her eyes.

6. Joe was sure all was not right, and he said: "We will go and see about it, Nanny."

7. "Ba-a-a!" said the sheep.

8. Joe went with her to the wood, and there was Nanny's own little white lamb with its head caught in the bushes.

9. Joe took it and put it by its mother.

10. "Ba-a-a-a!" said Nanny. She meant, "Thank you, dear Joe!"

24. LADY BUG.

gärden   rŏcked   Bŭg

hŏney   stĕms

                       līght

                       clōver

                       lēaves

                       lăntern

tälked   quīte

coūsin   âir   cāke

sŭpper   bĕd   slĕpt

Lädy   Bee   bush

---

b-u̯-sh   bush   s-t-ĕ-m-ş   stems

b-ŭ-ḡ   bug

---

1. Lady Bug lived on a rose-bush in our garden.

2. In the day time she walked up and down the green stems to get the air.

3. At night she slept on a soft bed of pink rose-leaves.

4. One fine day Lady Bug went to see her cousin, Miss Bee.

5. Miss Bee lived in a nice white house on the other side of the garden.

6. They rocked on the grass-stems, and talked for a long time.

7. Then they had clover cake and honey for their supper.

8. When it was time for Lady Bug to go home, it was quite dark.

9. "O, dear! What shall I do?" said she, "I can not see which way to go."

10. Just then, cousin Fire-Fly came in.

11. "Wait, Lady Bug," said he, "and I will light my lantern, and go home with you."

12. "Thank you, cousin, you are very kind," said Lady Bug.

25. TAKING CARE OF BABY.

knĕlt	shoes	replȳ	whīle
togĕther	cŭnning	once	märket
alŏne	enoŭgh	flo͞or	rōlled
cătch	hōld	Jūne	cǫuld

1. "Mary, can you take care of baby while I go to market?"

2. That is what Mary's mother said to her one fine June day.

3. "Yes, mamma, I think I am old enough to take care of baby. So go to the market and do not fear for us."

4. That is what Mary said in reply; and then mamma left the two alone together.

5. Mary took her little ball, tied a string to it, and rolled it along the floor.

6. Baby tried to catch it, and how he did laugh when he got hold of it.

7. "Why, baby, you have got off one of your shoes," said Mary.

8 Then she knelt down and put on his shoe.

9. When her mother came from market, this is what Mary said:

10. "Baby has not cried once; he has been just as good and cunning as could be. I like to take care of him."

Copy, and fill the blanks.

Mary took her —— and rolled it on the floor.

"Laugh, baby, laugh!" she ——, and how baby did ——.

26. A PICTURE LESSON.

Make a conversation lesson about this picture. In-quire what the children are doing; why they are showing their hands to their mother; whether they appear to be going away; where they appear to be going; what shows where they are going, etc.

27. SCRIPT REVIEW.

At Home, Thursday Eve.

Dear Papa,

    I have just read the last lesson in my First Reader.

    O, how glad I am, for mamma says I may go to school, if you are willing.

    One day I went to school with Miss Kate. I was only four, then, and cried to come home.

    Now I am seven, and nearly as tall as May.

    Please say yes, papa.

    From your loving little girl.

      Grace.